I0518901

The Covington Witches
Book of Secrets
Volume 1

A NOVEL BY
ROZ CARTER

Produced by Black, Brown and Beige Publishing

Philadelphia, PA

publisher@covingtonwitches.com

CHAPTER ONE

Philly

"No, no no no no not today." Imara ran to the oven from the far end of the kitchen holding the phone against her ear.

"Well, I told her that I don't want to go to church with her but she never listens to anything I say anyway."

Imara nodded her head as though her cousin Sabrina could see her. "Uh huh," she said, to let Sabrina know she was still paying attention.

Reaching the double oven, she pulled it open and was greeted by the aroma of crispy cheese on her baked ziti. "Shit," she muttered under her breath, imagining the dramatics she would have to deal with if she tried to serve the dish at the event this afternoon.

"Sweetie, I'm going to have to call you back. I've got a little problem to take care of right now, okay?"

Sabrina chuckled. "Sweetie is my mom, but okay, I'll let you go. Are you sure everything is okay? Anything on fire?" She laughed in the interim while waiting for Imara to hear what she actually said. It was amusing to think that Imara could have actually set anything on fire or created anything less than delicious in her catering kitchen. Everyone in the family relied on Imara for her beautiful cakes and pies during holidays, always beautifully yet simply, decorated with that extra little something in every bite.

The corner of Imara's mouth turned up in a reasonable facsimile of a smile at her cousin's quip. She massaged her left eyebrow with one hand while gesturing towards the large tray of ziti on the counter with the other. "No, nothing's on fire, very funny. A little crispy around the edges maybe, but no flames. Still, I better go, I may have to whip up another tray of ziti for the Baker party tonight though."

"Okay, but can we expect you at the house tomorrow for dinner?"

They both laughed, knowing what Imara's answer would be.

"No, I'm going to pass, I have some reading I want to do tomorrow night."

"Okay, but you are the only woman I know who makes a date with herself to read. Bye."

"Bye."

Imara placed the phone on the shelf below the stainless steel countertop and turned her attention to the ziti. *Who had baked ziti in the middle of summer anyway?* Ms. Baker loved ordering off menu, thinking with her stomach rather than her head, even when it meant serving her guests a heavy pasta dish in the heat of August.

"Huh, that's funny, I thought imore burnt than that," she said aloud. The ziti that she thought was too browned and crispy around the edges when she'd removed it from the oven looked practically perfect now.

"Talking to yourself is the first sign."

Her cousin Marla sashayed into the industrial kitchen, hanging her floppy tote bag on the hook by the door. Walking over to the sink to wash her hands, she glanced over at Imara, raising her right eyebrow.

"What's wrong now? Did the crazy Ms. Baker call and change her mind? Are we supposed to have dinner for 40 now?"

"No, nothing like that. I thought I'd burnt the ziti, but its fine."

"Of course it's fine. When do you ever cook anything that isn't fine?"

Shaking her head at her cousin, who she thought suffered from a severe case of perfectionism, Marla moved to the refrigerator to pull out some Parmesan.

"I don't need Parmesan for this." Imara said, looking up from the list of things she had to check off for the party.

"You may not need it, but I do; I'm starving!" Marla broke off a chunk from the block, haphazardly re-wrapped the larger block and placed it back in the refrigerator. Imara thought, *I'll re-wrap that when she leaves the kitchen; it's going to dry out otherwise.*

Walking towards the doorway, Marla slung her huge bag over her shoulder and said, "Chop, chop, time's a ticking. Let's get a move on, otherwise you're going to be late. Ms. Baker would love to call me to get something off her bill because you were five minutes later than the agreed upon time."

"I know," she said. Imara found Ms. Baker extremely unpleasant to deal with but her company had events often, so she had to grin and bear her antics, even if it killed her.

Imara finished the inventory for the guys to begin loading up the van, and placed the clipboard next to the stack of glassware. She pulled off her apron and dropped it into the hamper that was located in the alcove by the door. Imara picked up her iPhone and walked out of the kitchen after taking one last look around to make sure she hadn't forgotten anything. She was hungry but didn't have time to eat anything now. Imara knew she'd have to grab something when she got upstairs otherwise she'd be hungry and angry or hangry as Marla called it, by the end of the evening. *Oh, the Parmesan.* Imara walked back to the refrigerator and pulled out the cheese, and carefully re-wrapped it. It smelled delicious but she wanted something crunchy, and crisp to nosh, something that hopefully would stave off the headache that was threatening to develop.

She walked to the office down the hall and leaned in. Imara was always struck by the contrast between the pristine kitchen, her domain, and the office that looked like a hurricane had hit it, which was Marla's domain.

Marla sat behind a desk that had piles of papers, which were topped with books, which had various office supplies perched on top of them, all creating a precarious mountain that looked as if it were just waiting to topple at any moment. Leaning back in her chair, she looked up from her iPad as she heard Imara approach.

"I will never understand how you can work like this, it's a mess.

Actually, it's worse than a mess, it looks like a lunatic asylum."

"Uh huh, well you worry about you, I'll do me. Now, get out of here and go change please."

Once Imara left, Marla turned back to her iPad and the calendar for next week's events. They had two dinner clients scheduled for Monday, one breakfast meeting on Tuesday and a full sit-down dinner with bartending and waitstaff scheduled for Friday. She knew she would be exhausted by Saturday, but the business was doing so well lately, who was she to complain? Her cousin was getting some repeat clients and word of mouth was spreading in the community. Their catering business was professionally run and the food was always generously portioned and delicious, so business was booming.

The electric and gas bills had come in the other day. *Now, where were they?* Marla knew that if she started moving things from one pile to the other she could have a mess on her hands, if everything started to slide. She wanted to get out of here and get home so as she looked out of the door of the office, to see if anyone was around, she mouthed a few words. If anyone had been looking her way, it would have appeared as if she was saying a little prayer, especially when she closed her eyes briefly and dipped her head. When she opened her eyes, on top of the pile of paper to her left she spied the two pieces of mail she'd been searching for all along. "Ah, so that's where you were hiding," she said as she took her seat. Sitting down, she brought up the calendar once again and entered the due dates for each of the bills, humming tunelessly to herself.

She noticed the time and picked up her phone to give her cousin Chike a call.

"Do you plan on getting here anytime soon or should I tell Ms.

Baker that she should start screaming now?" Marla said as she heard the gruff "Hello," more statement than question, on the other end of the line.

"Marla, leave me alone. I'm on my way now."

"Fine. Bite my head off. I'm just trying to keep everything running smoothly around here." Marla ended the call, rolling her eyes.

Marla heard the garage door opening in the back of the warehouse on the kitchen side and breathed a sigh of relief. Chike got on her last nerve but he was a good guy and worked hard. It couldn't have been easy as the only male cousin in their generation. And any man that could put up with the crazy females in their family had to be a saint. Or something.

Imara turned and walked quickly down the hallway toward the freight elevator. As she pushed the button, she shifted her weight from foot to foot, willing the elevator to get there faster. She stepped into the elevator and untucked her shirt from her waistband. Even when she was cooking, she liked to look neat. On more than one occasion a client had stopped in unexpectedly and since the office was off limits, due to the way it looked, like a disaster area, she met with them in the little seating area at the front of the kitchen. As a bit of a germaphobe, Imara didn't like people to enter the kitchen without washing their hands. Asking strangers to do so at a first meeting would be out of the question, especially if she wanted to charge them the healthy prices that she did. So, the cafe table was the perfect spot for quick meetings.

She left the elevator and dropped her phone on the table in the entryway to her loft. The scent of sandalwood greeted her as she entered her apartment, followed by a pleasantly plump feline.

"Hello Amla, how's my baby?" She bent down and blew air kisses at her companion. Amla raised her head to return the greeting, purring loudly, a low, slow motor. Amla immediately tried to trip Imara as she walked toward her bedroom. As light on her feet as a cat, Imara caught herself from falling and rushed toward the bathroom.

Imara passed through the living room which was decorated in cool blues and light green, the space was dominated by a large green velvet Chesterfield sofa and floor to ceiling windows on one side that let in the light. As she walked down the long hallway to the back of the loft, she passed walls covered with artwork. Some were her creations, paintings and woven wall-hangings she had made, interspersed with pieces she had picked up in galleries, thrift stores and flea markets over the years. The only thing she looked for in art was that it made her feel something when she looked at it. If she could afford it she bought it. Imara made it to the bathroom and after relieving her bladder and washing her hands with her favorite hand-milled lavender scented soap, Imara took a moment to look in the mirror over the green glass basin. She could see the effects of the tension she felt on her face. She realized she was clenching her teeth so she opened her mouth widely to remove some of the tension from her jaw. She left the bathroom and went into the bedroom.

Her bedroom was her oasis. Bright with shades of orange and yellow, her bedroom made her happy. She kept the furnishings to a minimum but had a love of textiles.

There were small brightly colored quilts on the small loveseat and folded at the foot of her bed and thrown over the chair by her closet. She liked to run her fingers over the small neat stitches on the surface of the quilts; she admired the craftsmanship of the hand-sewn and embroidered quilts made by women a half a world away.

She opened the closet door on the right, where she kept the many copies of her work uniform of black slacks, and white shirts. She threw the clothes on the burnt orange slipper chair that sat next to her closet and kicked off her shoes on the way back to the bathroom. Imara turned the shower on full blast and waited for the room to fill with steam. She massaged the back of her neck, where there resided a knot of tension.

If she were honest with herself, she'd admit that she was tired, bone tired and needed a day or three off. She had been going non-stop for weeks now and really needed a little break from her very successful but stressful business. Sometimes she felt like a hamster on one of those stupid wheels, running on and on with no destination in sight and some bizarre absentee task master chuckling at her inane efforts. She loved cooking, she loved setting up events, styling her food, watching people enjoying her food. Sometimes when people half-closed their eyes in pleasure from her food, it gave her a real thrill. All of those things she loved. What she didn't love was the back-breaking schedule that they'd had this summer, the dinner events followed by breakfast meeting setups, followed sometimes by dinner events on the same night.

She made a mental note to look over the schedule for September with Marla tomorrow. Thankfully they didn't have an event this weekend. The thought of waking early to do prep work was enough to make her tense all over again.

Imara leaned her forehead against the shower tiles and let the hot water beat down on her head. She could feel the knot at the base of her neck loosening under the needles of hot water. Breathing deeply, she counted to ten. She stepped reluctantly from the shower, dried off briskly and moved to quickly dress for work.

She was just slipping the small pearls into her ears when her phone vibrated with a text. Imara ignored it, thinking it was probably Marla, the taskmaster, hurrying her along, she slipped into her shoes and headed towards the elevator putting the phone into her pocket. She felt it vibrating against her thigh as she pressed the button to go downstairs.

"Oh for godssake, I'm on my way down." She pulled the phone from her pocket to write a snarky text to Marla when she saw the messages were from her Aunt Cairi.

Know you're on the way to work. Call me when you finish. No matter how late. I'm fine, just call, family needs you.

Nope, not today. What now? Imara was annoyed with her favorite auntie. The last thing she needed right now was more pressure. What she needed was a break. She resisted the urge to text back a terse "**what?**" because she needed to stay focused on the event ahead.

As she stepped off of the elevator, family issues dropped away and she was all business, all her business.

CHAPTER TWO

Edenton

As she ended the call with her aunt, Imara absentmindedly continued to pet Amla. She was still a little stunned. Just last night while she was in the shower she had been lamenting how she needed a break. It seemed she was about to get an extended break. She was headed to a town that she'd never been to before, Edenton, North Carolina, the birthplace of her mother and aunts. And her great grandmother Nawnie, too, she supposed.

Her mind was running all over the place. She had so much to do in such a short amount of time, if she thought about it too long, she'd wonder how she'd gotten roped into representing the family at this funeral for some great uncle that she'd never met. Apparently her aunties couldn't bear to leave town right now and were calling on the younger generation to represent the Philly branch of the family at the funeral. God forbid no one from Philly actually go; that thought never entered into the equation. No, they, Aunties Cairi and Sweetie had talked it over after they'd received news that Uncle Brownlee had died. They'd also decided that she, and her cousins Chike and Cat should be the ones to go. Never mind that they were no longer children who could be picked up and placed wherever the "adults" needed them to be. Never mind that she and Chike had work to do for her catering business and that Cat had private duty clients to care for. No, all concerns went out the window when a family matter came up. And now it was their turn to drop everything and do their duty.

Secretly she thought it was a heaven-sent opportunity and was happy to leave town for a day or two. The only real problems were the events she had scheduled for next week. Of course Aunt Cairi had taken care of that also, enlisting Charlotte to handle the catering events in her stead. Charlotte could cook, *but* if she thought about it there was always something not right about her dishes. Imara thought she was just being a perfectionist, but it was weird how everything Charlotte cooked tasted, *bitter,* even her cookies. Imara shook her head. She was being silly and a control freak, everyone thought Charlotte was a good cook. Imara had never heard anyone in the family describe Charlotte's food as bitter, besides, Imara had no other choice. She'd rather have a good cook take over the events than cancel all of the events for next week. And, Marla had offered to help Charlotte with the dishes, which was so nice of her. She really had the best cousins and family in the world. They really knew what the meaning of family was all about.

When Imara thought of the two of them, Charlotte, a recipe follower to the "T" and Marla, who had an aversion to any rules, including the chemistry rules of baking, working side by side to put out the dishes, she grinned and cringed at the same time. They'd work it out. Somehow.

Now she had Marla by way of Aunt Cairi to thank for one less thing to think about; she'd even booked their Amtrak tickets, for her, Chike and Cat, so all she had to do was pack.

She thought about going down South in the middle of August and some of her happy feelings slipped away. *And wasn't Edenton a swamp? That meant hot and sticky right?* She picked up her phone to call Cat. Of the three of them she was the only one who had ever been to Edenton, for a family reunion a few years ago.

"Hey cuz." Cat's sultry voice that reminded one of molasses sliding slowly over a spoon; she always sounded like she had been awakened from a nice nap.

"Hey, what's the weather like there?"

"Well, that's a good question. Imara, meet Google or Weather,.com or the 21st century. How am I supposed to know what the weather is like? Look it up." Cat said all of this with a slightly bemused tone, but it still made Imara feel stupid.

"Oh, yeah. I guess I could do that," Imara said, laughing at herself. "I just thought it was worth asking you since you'd been there before. Sorry, I'm an idiot. Are you packed yet?"

"No, I'm sure it's a thousand degrees there, but, most of the people actually have air conditioning. But, knowing how backwoods some of the family is, maybe you shouldn't count on the air conditioning."

"Are you serious?" Imara was shocked to consider that there might be people living without air conditioning in this day and age and in the South, in a swamp at that. She pulled flowy cottony dresses with flat sandals from her closet and threw them into her bag. Maybe she should bring a sweater or two, just in case.

"Oh, yes, I'm very serious." You know those people have special blood or something, the heat doesn't bother them like it does us Northerners. At least you'll finally get to see the family place."

"Yeah, I actually am excited about that. Although it's kind of sick to think it had to be a death in the family to get me to go."

Always pragmatic, Cat snorted, "Eh, people die, I think he was really old? I don't exactly remember him but yeah, the important thing is getting there. I think you'll like it. After the culture shock."

"Oh my god, Cat, I have left the city before, I just have been busy building my business for the past few years."

"Yes, and as a result, you go nowhere and do nothing but work, day in and day out. It's so…normal of you to live like that."

"What do you mean by normal? I'm just as weird as the rest of you. I just like working that's all. I'm creating something here. Not everyone can jet off to the islands at the drop of a hat."

"Actually, cuz, they can. They just think they can't. If I'm going to be ready when you come over here in a few minutes, let me go so I can throw this stuff in my bag and put on some comfortable clothes for this long train ride."

"Okay. I'll be there soon. Is Chike ready?"

"Probably, I haven't seen him. See you soon."

Imara could hear the elevator making it's way up to her floor. As she heard the door open she shouted to the front of the loft "I'm getting out of town, I'm getting out of town. Ah hah, I'm leaving all the work to you and Charlotte and I'm getting out of Dodge." The smile died on her lips when she turned around and saw Charlotte, unsmilingly standing behind her.

"Oh, I thought you were Marla, hah." Imara noticed Charlotte did not look happy. She didn't look angry either, she just looked, *bitter.* There was that word again. What was her cousin bitter about she wondered.

"Charlotte are you okay? Are you sure you can fit in doing the events for me? I really appreciate it. I was just telling Cat, that truth be told, I'm glad for the excuse to get out of town for a few."

"Yeah, it must be nice. Nah, seriously though, you deserve it, you are a hard-working woman. And you don't do anything for fun, ever. It's no problem for me, plus, how could I say no, Auntie Cairi and my mother would never hear of it. I'll just stay up all hours of the day and night to get everything done." Charlotte looked at Imara then down at the floor.

Following family tradition, Charlotte worked in one of the family businesses. Her regular job was working in Sweetie's health food store. Imara thought she was in charge of inventory and accounts receivable. Other than a very small number of support staff, everyone who worked for the various Covington businesses were related either by blood or marriage. As a result, sometimes the cousins had more than one job at a time, because rather than give it to an outsider, it was tradition to just fill in the slack and keep the money in the family. It made for a very insular existence, but since most everyone got along, it was something they were all used to. Besides, if someone did have a problem with the way things were, who were they going to cross, one of the Aunties? Not likely to happen. So, in situations like this, the best person, meaning the one deemed right for the job at the moment, took up any slack in a family emergency or situation.

Death always took precedence over marriages. There weren't too many of those in the family, nowadays. The various odd cousin here or there would decide to marry and then they would either do the lobster thing, and mate for life, or it would dissolve or blow up in a year or two.

As these ideas flitted through her mind she looked at her cousin. Imara wondered if Charlotte's marriage was in trouble and headed for the dumpster. Truth be told, Imara found Charlotte's husband James, unpleasant and rather creepy.

He always stared about four seconds too long for normal when she or anyone had a conversation with him; plus, he had a slow blink which she found odd. When Charlotte first introduced him to the family, Imara remembered giggling with her cousin Chike about Mr. Long-Stare. They had been overheard by her Auntie Cairi, Chike's mother. When asked if she had noticed anything wrong with James, Cairi just shook her head and said "He is beyond help, poor thing." Which did nothing to stop Imara and Chike from thinking there was something wrong with him after all. After Charlotte and James had gotten married it seemed that even more life and vitality had left James. He had grayed within months and often seemed drunk or out of it at family gatherings. And it was obvious that Charlotte was the head of that household.

"Char, how's James, I haven't seen him in awhile?"

"Oh, he's fine. Getting on my nerves, plus, he was busy this summer. I keep him busy, otherwise he's all under my feet all day. I'll be glad when school starts again in a couple of weeks so he can get out of my hair."

"Oh, Charlotte, I forgot to even ask you, why'd you stop by?"

"Oh, I just wanted to know if there was anything you needed me to do while you were gone besides feed Miss Fatty?"

Imara always took offense when people called her cat fat, and she was sure it was a family joke and that's why they did it.

"No, I can't think of anything. Marla can go over the menu stuff for the three events with you, and I'm sure I'll be checking in from time to time. But, thank you Charlotte, you're a good cousin for helping out like this, I really appreciate it."

"No problem, my pleasure to help out."Charlotte smiled her lopsided smile and went to hug her cousin, rubbing her on the back. Her hand left a slight smudge, barely visible on the back of Imara's white shirt as they parted.

Imara barely noticed the slight crunch of dust under her shoe as she passed the threshold of her apartment as they entered the elevator.

Imara and Charlotte got into separate cars, Imara heading towards Covington House, Charlotte on her way to Center City to Reading Terminal to pick up something for dinner for James and herself.

Covington House was only a few blocks from her apartment and she didn't bother to get out of the car. As much as she loved her aunts, sometimes if they were at home it was never a quick in and out.

Instead, she texted Cat - **Outside. Ready?**

They had over an hour before the train left and even if the expressway was backed up, they were sure to get there in plenty of time. During normal traffic, the ride from West Germantown to 30th Street Station was about 15 minutes away.

No response from Cat, which could mean either she had lain her phone down somewhere in the sprawling house and had no idea she had received a text. Or, more plausibly, she was running late *and* had lost the phone somewhere. Either way, Imara would go up to the door as a last resort. She texted Chike, - **Ready? I'm outside. Hurry up.**

This time she received a response - **Ready, but Mom wants you to come in for a min.**

Imara groaned, but turned off the car anyway and opened the door. She knew better than to try to argue with her Auntie Cairi. She made her way toward the house.

Covington House, like the other houses on the block, was set back from the street. Unlike the other houses, it was a sprawling, ostentatious affair, built in the French palatial style popular in the late 1890s. The house sat on a few acres, which was unusual for a home within the city, let alone in the neighborhood of West Germantown. The house had turrets, and rounded wings and set back areas. There was a large front porch a side porch on the east side and a back porch as well.

Many of the rooms had balconies on the back of the house and it had more rooms than Imara had ever thought to count. She had grown up there and it never occurred to her that it was strange that most of her family lived in the same house. The house was so large that it never felt crowded, even when everyone was gathered for holidays, or various family celebrations. When family visited from out of town, there was never a question as to where they would stay, it was always at Covington House. At any given time, there might be cousins or aunts in the house that she might not even know were in attendance until they passed one another in a hallway.

The front lawn was lush with green grass and flower beds on either side of the walkway. The gardens were her Aunt Cairi's special project. She was an avid gardener. The back of the house was a wild space with more flowers, trees and herbs than Imara could identify. Her aunt had a special knack for growing anything and if Imara needed a special herb for a dish, she could count on her aunt having some in her gardens.

The garden beds on the front and side lawns were looking particularly lush in the August heat. As you approached the house the air became redolent with the scents of sweet flowers and herbs. The trees that framed the sides of the house provided much needed shade dropping the temperature near the house about ten to fifteen degrees.

Imara saw two women at the table on the lawn near the east side of the house, having coffee or tea. Unable to make out who it was from this distance, she just raised her hand in greeting and walked up onto the porch. Two little kids, she thought they belonged to her cousin Shay, a boy and a girl about five years old were in the corner, playing quietly. They looked like they were petting one of her aunts cats to death, with the heavy handed love of a young child. "Hi Imara!", they shouted almost in unison, their little brown faces shiny with the heat of summer and childhood. Imara, keenly aware of the clock that was ticking away in the back of her head, ran bent over towards them and reached her hands out to tickle them, she ran away to the front door as the children doubled over in exaggerated delight.

She opened the huge oak door and walked into the hushed silence of Covington House. Cool air moving from right to left seemed to caress her face as she stood in the foyer. She stood for a moment before calling out and listened to the sounds coming from the various parts of the house and from the house itself.

Imara always found herself listening to the house and she imagined it always had something to say to her. Today the energy of the house seemed low, a low hum that was barely perceptible, running right below the surface of consciousness.

A large round room, it was dominated by four large ten foot windows that flooded the room with light. She found her Aunt Cairi sitting in a wingback chair near one of the windows, her feet up on an old brocade ottoman.

Her Aunt Cairi was a woman in her mid-sixties, her rounded face belying her age. The only markers of age were a few crow's feet around her eyes and the laugh lines framing her wide mouth. Her long locs were threaded with silver and characteristically piled atop her head in an elaborate updo. Cairi was wearing "house clothes" a loose short sleeve cotton top with squared neckline in dark green and a flowy skirt in denim that had seen better days, faded and worn. Her feet were bare on the ottoman, but her flip flops were sitting next to them, ready for her feet to slide into them.

Cairi had the type of face that caused people, even strangers, to have long conversations with her, in stores, waiting rooms and while waiting in line at the supermarket. Cairi wasn't as nice as she appeared. Stubborn and domineering at times, she could be tough as nails and even fearsome when crossed. There weren't many in the family who crossed Cairi, preferring to do as she asked rather than face her wrath, even though her wrath was more often a withering look than a raised voice. Imara remembered being in the house when her Aunt Cairi and Uncle Gray were arguing as a child. Sure, there were slammed doors, but more often their arguments were characterized by chilly silences that lasted for days at a time. Imara smiled slightly thinking of her Uncle Gray. She missed him terribly. A bear of a man, when he hugged you, you were good and hugged. He had been dead for little over two years and she could spy on her aunt's face when she was thinking of her long-standing partner, Cairi would get a far off look and most often would shake her head as if remembering a shared joke with her husband. They were an impressive couple, both tall and broad of shoulder, they were stately. Her aunt with her long gray locs, her uncle with his broad brown face with the deep frown lines above his bushy eyebrows.

"Thought you were going to get out of coming in to say goodbye before leaving?" Cairi's voice was low and husky, a mixture of smoke and whiskey. She looked at Imara, her eyes kind, a slight smile playing at the corners of her wide mouth.

"No, I knew I couldn't be so lucky. Oh, my, god, where are Chike and

Cat? Seriously, we need to leave, I'm not even joking now."

"Will you calm down, we're right here." Chike walked into the room a duffel bag slung over each shoulder and pulling a rolling suitcase that Imara hoped belonged to Cat. It was purple leather, and looked like alligator. He dumped the bags by the door and walked over to his mother, bending over to kiss her on her plump cheek.

"Be good while we're gone, I'll call you when we get to the house."

"Bye Auntie, tell my mother we had to leave before she could get back," Cat called from the hallway, pulling a tan jacket on over her black tank dress. Cat looked a lot like her mother, Imara's Aunt Sweetie, and little like her sister Charlotte. Where Charlotte often had a severe look on her face, an "evil look"as Uncle Gray used to tease, Cat was always smiling. Where Charlotte was light-skinned with a smattering of freckles across her nose and cheeks and had light brown hair with reddish highlights, Cat was closer in complexion to Imara, medium brown skinned with an aquiline nose and full lips, her face was a symphony of contradictions. Cat was perpetually in a good mood and eager to laugh. Finding the world around her amusing, even though she was only in her early thirties, she already had deeper laugh lines than her Aunt Cairi, who was twice her age.

"Bye Cat, be good," Cairi called from the living room. Cat laughed as she walked onto the porch. Imara leaned over to kiss Cairi goodbye. Cairi caught her eye and gave her a long look before saying, "Bye, give everybody our condolences. I think you'll find Edenton...interesting. You sleep on the train. You need it. Chike, make sure y'all call me when you get to Ora's house. I want to know what the flowers look like. Somebody take a picture."

Chike and Imara laugh at that last comment, as they leave the house. "What's she going to do, post the pic to Instagram?"

"You know her, she probably will. Probably just wants to make sure she has the biggest arrangement, that's all, you know my mom."

Cat was already in the backseat, checking her makeup in her hand mirror.

"Cat, you're beautiful, as always, nothing's changed." Imara knew her cousin was vain, unable to pass a mirror without checking her reflection and almost always delighted with what she saw. Pursing her lips, doing "duck face", Cat smoothed imaginary lines from her forehead.

As she pulled away from the house, Imara could have sworn she saw the curtain twitch in one of the upstairs windows. She thought it was Nawnie's room, but that was unlikely. Her great-grandmother spent most of her days sitting in her rocker. Yes, it was positioned by the window, but she didn't move around much, preferring to be waited on by the various great-grandchildren. Imara was being unfair. Nawnie was at least 102 years old, if she didn't deserve to be waited on, Imara couldn't imagine who did. Imara often wondered if her great grandmother was fooling them all with her silent act. Whenever Imara went to talk to her, the conversations were one-sided, but Nawnie still smiled or raised an eyebrow, responding to points in the conversation, making it known that she was aware of what was being said.

Leaving thoughts of Covington House, West Germantown and the business behind, the three cousins retreated to their own thoughts as Imara sped on the expressway, heading towards the train station.

Once they were situated on the train, Chike pulled out his iPad to read, while Cat pulled out her mirror to check her makeup.

"What in the world do you think changed from the last time you checked your face?" Chike said. Chike had very little time for his vain cousin, thinking her foolish in her obsession with her looks.

Cat just laughed, ignoring Chike's jabs.

Imara sat across from her cousins and looked at Chike.

Dressed in dark washed jeans and a dark blue linen shirt, Chike was simplicity personified. Imara realized even his sandals were dark blue leather. A gentle giant, Chike favored his father in looks and mannerisms, at over six feet five inches, he had broad shoulders, a narrow waist and huge hands. The color of dark chocolate, he had thick features, thick eyebrows, wide, deep-set eyes a wide nose and wide, full lips. His dark complected face was framed by a neatly trimmed beard and mustache that lately was showing more salt mixed with the pepper. Imara watched as he reached into his shirt pocket to pull out his glasses.

"Since when do you wear glasses?"

"You really do walk around in a fog don't you?" Cat shook her head at her cousin's tunnel vision.

"No, seriously, *Chike,* when'd you get glasses?" Imara paid no attention to Cat. She saw Chike everyday at the catering shop, the glasses had to be new, or she would have noticed them before today, right?

"I got them about a month ago."

"He doesn't really need them, I don't know why he didn't just ask his mother for something."

Chike looked out of the corner of his eye at Cat sitting beside him, one corner of his mouth turned up. "Yeah, mom can really cure old age. Don't believe everything your Auntie tells you Cat. You're sounding a little naive, don't you think?"

Chike's mother was known for her teas and broths, known to cure everything from headaches to gout.

Imara knew that most of the ingredients came from Cairi's prolific gardens. She even had a drying shed on the property, festooned with bundles of drying herbs and flowers. If Cairi couldn't be found in the house, she could most likely be found in the drying shed, which even boasted a fireplace, so that she would be comfortable in all seasons.

Chike went back to reading his book on his iPad, hoping that something or someone would soon distract Cat, so that he could finish his book in peace and quiet. *Cat was like a small child at times,* thought Chike. He was certain that pretty soon a shiny new object would come into view to turn her attention away from the conversation at hand.

And as if by magic, a tall man in his mid-thirties was making his way down the aisle toward them. Like a heat-seeking missile Cat locked eyes with him and sat a little straighter in her seat. She lifted her chest and dropped her chin so that when she looked up at her target, her eyes appeared huge.

"I'm going to the dining car, anybody want anything?" Before Chike and Imara could answer, Cat had gotten out of her seat and was walking towards the next car, walking directly in front of her target.

Chike shook his head at his cousin's antics. He knew that it would be awhile before they saw Cat and that when she returned she'd be flushed with the success of her latest conquest.

Imara reached down to the bag on the floor at her feet to pull out a hardcover book.

"Wow, how old school of you. Don't you have an iPad?" Chike asked.

"I like to read cookbooks in real, dead tree book form. Sometimes I even turn down the corners."

By the time Cat returned, ostensibly from the dining car, carrying three bottles of water, Imara was sound asleep and Chike was nodding off, legs stretched out in front of him, iPad perilously perched on his stomach.

Imara woke up a few minutes before the train pulled into Union Station. The conductor had been through the car to let everyone know that there would be a wait of thirty minutes while the engines were switched in D.C.

Cat and Imara left Chike sleeping and got off the train to stretch their legs.

"I remember taking the train down South when I was younger and this platform would be filled with people who were smoking." Cat looked around at the few people who were standing around. "Now everybody is a zombie, fascinated by whatever they're looking at on their phones."

"Well, I'd rather be surrounded by zombies than cigarette smoke." Imara leaned against one of the columns, looking at the so-called zombies. She had to admit it was strange to see everyone with their heads hanging forward staring blankly at the tiny screens in front of their faces.

"I want a cigarette," Cat announced suddenly.

"You're not actually going to buy a pack of cigarettes, are you?" Imara asked, her eyes widening in surprise. "Besides, it's boiling out here, it's too hot to smoke".

"Watch, and learn," Cat said as she walked toward a man at the other end of the platform. He was standing alone, puffing on a cigarette, banished to the end of the platform, away from polite society.

Imara shook her head at Cat's antics. *Cat is nothing but a bundle of impulses held together with hair and legs.* Cat had reached the man at the end of the platform and was saying something to him; they were too far away for Imara to hear the conversation, but she could imagine the content. Cat, smiling, laid her left hand on the man's right arm. He reached into his back pocket and held out the pack for her. With her hand still on his arm and looking up at him, Cat extracted a cigarette from the pack. Never taking his eyes off of her, the man lit her cigarette, seeming to be under her spell.

Bored with the scene her cousin was playing out, Imara looked at the other people around her to see if anything else worthwhile was happening. The family to her left was fairly silent, each of the four members interacting with their phones. The mother, a woman in her early forties, wearing shorts that pinched her thick thighs and a cheap looking short sleeved shirt looked up at Imara, with an angry look on her face. Imara, not understanding where the anger was coming from and not knowing why the nameless woman was directing it at her, stared back at the hausfrau, keeping her face blank. When the woman took too long to look away, Imara slightly raised her right eyebrow, and the woman looked away with a sharp intake of breath.

"Making friends I see," Chike said, startling her.

"You scared me half to death! Don't sneak up on me like that." Imara said, her hand rising to her throat.

Chike smiled and looked around. "Where'd Cat slink off to?"

"Oh, she decided she needed to smoke a cigarette," Imara said, tipping her head in the direction she'd last seen Cat with the Cigarette Man.

"Of course she did," Chike said, "Do I have time to get a sandwich?"

"Yeah, we don't pull off for another 10 minutes. You can get one if you hurry."

Chike was halfway to the escalator, his long legs striding along the platform.

Imara made her way back to the train and their seats, settling back wondering if she'd be able to fall back to sleep. The nap had been so refreshing. She realized it had probably been a year since she'd taken a nap in the middle of the day. Her days for the past three years were filled with the tasks of building her catering business, *Imara's Kitchen*. Naps were a luxury, something her cat Amla was able to indulge in, but not her. The lights in the car went off then on again, and then there was a hum. She wondered if she should text her cousins. As she pulled out her phone, she saw Chike striding along the platform. He passed two teen girls who couldn't seem to pull their eyes from him as he walked towards, then past them. Chike, as usual, was seemingly oblivious to the female attention. Cat was nowhere to be seen. Chike slid into his seat and looked down the aisle.

"Should we leave her?" he said, a mischievous look in his eyes.

"No, I have a feeling she might not like that too much. I'm going to text her."

"Where are you? The train is not going to wait for you"

After what seemed like several minutes with no response from Cat, Imara punched in her number. The phone rang, then Cat answered, breathlessly saying, "I'm coming. I'll be right there." With that she hung up the phone.

What seemed like five minutes passed; Cat came running down the aisle.

"You're on the train, why are you still running?" Chike asked looking at her suspiciously.

"Is someone chasing you? What's wrong?" Imara asked.

Cat smiling, looking like the cat that swallowed the canary, said, "Whew, I'm getting too old to run!"

"How'd you get rid of the smell? I was afraid you'd come back with your clothes reeking of cigarette smoke," Imara said as she opened her cookbook again. Maybe it would work as a sleeping pill again.

Cat snapped her fingers and said "Magic."

The remainder of the train ride was punctuated by periods of sleep and wakefulness, each of the cousins taking turns with each of the activities available to them on the train. For the remaining hours they were all three seldom awake all at the same time. When two of them happened to be awake at the same time they took the time for quick whispered conversations. Imara was fascinated by the changing scenery, the smaller and smaller towns that the train passed through. She couldn't imagine living in one of those places. She was a city girl through and through. The idea of spending her life knowing she would keep seeing the same few thousand people year in and year out was inconceivable. Even though her circle of friends, family and acquaintances was small, she had the potential to share her space with hundreds of thousands in her beloved city. The opportunity was there. The people existed, she could go downtown and be jostled from one street to the other, never seeing or being seen by anyone that she knew. There was comfort in the thought that she could disappear into the crowd if she wanted. That opportunity didn't exist living in a small town.

Imara was beginning to get restless. She looked over and saw Cat looking at her.

"What's wrong? Is my hair sticking up or something?"

"Nothing. Just thinking you've never been to Aunt Essie's home, that's all."

At the mention of her mother's name, Imara's heart skipped a beat. Even after all of these years, she couldn't believe how much she still missed her mother. She wondered if the day would ever come when she'd hear her mother mentioned and her heart wouldn't hurt. She hoped not.

"Nope, I've never seen Edenton. It's going to be *interesting* according to Aunt Cairi."

"Oh yeah, it'll be interesting, that's for sure. It always is." Cat grinned and looked out the window.

The landscape outside was green. Just expanses of green dotted by houses, usually painted white. They even passed a few cows moving only their jaws slowly chewing cud in the August heat.

Seven hours and three very numb butts later the train pulled into the station in Norfolk. Edenton was such a small town, that the closest train station was a state away, in Virginia. There was a rental car arranged for them at the train station.

Chike was glad to get moving, he was even glad to haul their luggage from the train to the trunk of the car. Each of his cousins took the opportunity to run to the ladies room while he did some stretches in the parking lot while looking at the directions on his phone. He thought he remembered how to get to Aunt Ora's from here, but it had been several years since he'd visited and the last thing he felt like doing after a seven hour train ride was to get lost in the wilds of North Carolina and he'd be damned if he asked anyone on the way. Not that they were likely to see anyone on the road to ask anyway. He hated driving through the South at night, he hated that he had a stupid rental car instead of his own reliable truck, which was sitting in the garage back at Covington House.

According to the map, it looked like a straight shot down US 17 from here to Edenton. They weren't likely to get lost once they were in Edenton town proper. The entire town was smaller than their neighborhood back in Philly. He took a deep breath of the humid Southern air *Fresh. That's what it smelled like.* He sent off a quick text to his girlfriend Evony - **in Chesapeake about to get on highway. Text when we get to Edenton.**

He and Evony had been together about four years. She was nice, fairly mellow but he knew she wasn't the one he would end up with. Evony worshipped the ground he walked on and that was one of the problems. He knew that some of it was beyond her control, but there was no way he was ever going to feel the same way about her. There was something missing, he knew what it was, she knew it was the case. Each was just waiting, biding their time until the thing that would end their relationship showed up. They were comfortable with one another at this point,but bored and too lazy to wreck their lives together with a breakup.

Evony was so mellow, she was probably just waiting for him to say something. He had a feeling their breakup would be amicable. He hoped that it would be, he didn't want to have to do anything to *make it* amicable. Rubbing his hands together in anticipation, he knew that even though the reason for their coming

South was the funeral for Uncle Brownlee, he really was in the mood for a little *fun,* family style.

When Imara and Cat came back, the three of them piled into the rental car with Chike behind the wheel and headed toward US 17 and Edenton.

Back home in Philly, gritty ill will kindled in rooms that were not quite empty.

Imara's first glimpse of Edenton was shrouded in darkness. That was something she couldn't get over, how deep the night seemed in the South. The surrounding trees absorbed whatever light was emitted by the few street lights and businesses on Broad Street. It really seemed like a place set back in time, but Imara thought that maybe that was because she hadn't seen the whole place by the light of day. She said as much to her cousins and they both got a hearty laugh.

"No, this is it, the town doesn't get any bigger by daylight. It's a one horse town without a horse." Chike said, not needing to really pay close attention to the road, because they were they only ones on it. "No horses, but, uh, plenty of horseflies and mosquitoes. It is a swamp, after all."

Cat wasn't looking out the window, her face was lit by the eerie bluish light of her iPad, where she was engrossed in a game involving getting water to a swamp creature.

Imara couldn't get a real sense of the town that night. She imagined there was more to the place than what she saw as they drove to Aunt Ora's house that night. Otherwise the entire town was smaller than her neighborhood, West Germantown, back in Philly. One thing she did notice was just how quiet it was. Less light pollution, less noise pollution, probably fewer people so, less pollution altogether. *It must be very boring here,* Imara thought, showing her Big City prejudiced. It made her smile to herself. In what felt like ten minutes since hitting the town, Chike pulled into the driveway of a house on the waterfront.

"Oh, it's so pretty. I wish I lived literally across the street from the water," Imara said as she got out of the car. Taking a full stretch, she looked at the water less than fifty feet from the house.It was dark, obviously, but there were a few lights glinting on the surface and she thought she could make out the smallest little island off to the right, big enough to have just two trees inhabiting it. Cat and Chike were at the door of the house. Before they could knock, it was opened by a huge man who filled the doorway. Standing well over six and a half feet tall, he looked like family. He had a similar shaped face with the family trait of wide mouths that broke into easy smiles and even easier laughs.

His hand was so big that Imara felt hers swallowed in his as he practically pulled her into the house.

The living room was filled with more relatives. Chike introduced the cousin who had greeted them at the door as Deon, and that introduction was followed by a flurry of names and faces that Imara barely tried to keep straight, let alone remember. She was always terrible at remembering names and thought she's probably spend the next few days with just a pleasant look on her face, that would hopefully hide the fact that she had no idea who she was speaking to.

She did remember to pay attention when Aunt Ora was introduced, she thought it would be rude not to recognize the woman whose house she was staying in and whose husband had just died.

When they were introduced she realized that her great uncle Brownlee had to have been ancient, the woman sitting before her was older looking than Nawnie, but that wasn't possible, was it? Maybe they were cousins, she and Nawnie. Imara was always hazy on family ties, especially when people were once removed or added by marriage. In truth, she didn't care that much, preferring to keep her circle of family and friends small. A natural introvert what was normally seen as standoffish behavior was simply Imara's way of conserving her energy. Large gatherings, like this one, drained her. Pretty soon she'd have to find a reason to excuse herself, just to catch her breath and collect her thoughts and to do nothing for a few minutes.

Aunt Ora was a gracious hostess, she asked one of the cousins to show Imara, Cat and Chike to their rooms. Ora got up from her chair and slowly made her way to the stairs in the large hallway. Moving like someone with hip or knee trouble, she took the stairs one at a time, so the four cousins, Imara, Cat, Chike and their cousin Nilah, waited until she was at the top to start up, so it wouldn't seem as if they were rushing the old woman.

Nilah and Cat were talking about the last time they had seen one another, their conversation punctuated by lots of laughter. It seemed they were good friends and kept in touch often. Imara paid very little attention to their conversation, just picking up snippets. She was more interested and impressed by the house.

Nilah took them up to the second floor. Imara could see that there was at least one more floor above them. The hallway was wide with doors on both sides and a large stained glass window at the far end. Imara didn't know what style the house was, just that the hardwood floors were beautiful and it looked like there were a few pieces of important artwork hanging on the walls. Chike was shown to his room first, his room closest to the second floor landing. Nilah showed Imara to a room in the middle of the hall on the right side.

"Make yourself comfortable, if you need anythin', just let one of us know. We're so glad you came! Even if it had to be for a funeral. But, Uncle Brownlee was old, so..." Nilah was smiling and looking intently at Imara, with a look of genuine delight in her eyes. Nilah's eyes twinkled. She had the look of someone who knew there was something amusing happening behind the scenes that she alone was privy to. "The bathroom is at the end of the hall on this side, or if somebody's in that one, there's one on the first floor near the kitchen. Or if you don't mind climbin' the stairs, there's one at the front of the house on the third floor. I put towels and stuff on the dresser there, but if you forgot somethin' just holla, we prob'ly have it. Oh, my God, I forgot to ask, y'all hungry?"

At the mention of food, Imara's stomach decided to answer for her, making a rude rumbling sound. "Uh, I guess I am. If it's okay, can I lay down for a minute and then get something to eat?" Imara asked, putting her suitcase on the floor beside the bed.

Her back was turned so she didn't see the look that Nilah and Cat exchanged. What she heard was, "Yes, of course. I can brang somethin' up to you too, you know. That way you don't even have to deal wit' all the folks downstairs. They a rowdy bunch and if you come back down, they'll never let you leave again tonight. Next thang you know, it'll be dawn and they'll still be talkin'." The idea was horrifying to Imara. "I don't want you to wait on me, seriously, I can just grab something out of the kitchen, even a handful of crackers and a slice of cheese and I'll be fine."

"Nope, I'll brang you up a sandwich. And something to drink. You want a glass of wine? We've got white, red, we got whiskey, just name it."

Imara said she'd take a sandwich with a glass of wine. She and Cat wished one another a good night. She thought the wine would help to relax her. Even though the house was very comfortable, she could still feel the closeness of the air, almost as a physical presence. She supposed it was the humidity, especially since the water was literally across the street.

While waiting for her cousin Nilah to come back, Imara looked around the room. There was a four poster bed, possibly an antique, framed by windows on each side. The windows were dressed with lovely white lace curtains. The bedspread was also white lace as well as the little doily on the back of the chair by the window. The decor felt very Southern to Imara. It didn't look like the decor had changed very much, if at all, in the past fifty years. Although the furnishings were very old, there was not a spot of dust anywhere. *I hope that old woman is not still cleaning her own house.*

Imara pulled the curtain back to see if she could see anything of the backyard. She was assisted by the moonlight. There was a grand backyard with a wide expanse of lawn and she could see a deck of some sort attached at the back of the house. The lawn lead to what looked like a lake in the back, overhung with trees and vines. The moon reflected on a body of water, but she couldn't tell how large it was or what lay beyond the water. She was surprised to learn the house had water to its front and back. She couldn't wait for tomorrow when she'd get a chance to look around in the daylight.

As she finished putting away her clothes in the dresser, there was a knock on the door. "Come in", Imara said. Nilah walked in carrying a tray with sandwiches, chips, cookies, a glass of orange juice, a bottled water and a bottle of white wine and another glass. Imara took the tray from her, laughing. "Oh my god, look at all of this food! Thank you." Imara shook her head at the bounty before her.

"I didn't know how hungry or thirsty you might be, so I just kept throwing stuff on the tray. Plus, you

might wake up and want a snack."
Nilah shrugged her shoulders.

"Well, thank you, I think I am set for the night. Now, don't judge if that whole tray is empty in the morning!" They both laughed and Nilah wished Imara a good night.

After finishing off most of the food and two glasses of wine, Imara felt stuffed and sleepy. She left the room to wash the travel grime from her face in the bathroom down the hall. She heard the low rumble of people still talking down stairs. Padding back to her room, she closed the door and heaved a sigh of relief. Eyeing the antique looking bedspread, she pulled it back and slipped between cool white sheets. Before her head had properly hit the pillow, she was snoring softly.

Sometime in the middle of the night, there came a soft knock on the door to Imara's room where she slept soundly. Not getting an answer, the door opened and a figure slipped inside, closing the door softly.

Nilah stood still for a moment waiting for her eyes to adjust to the deep darkness. She stood with her left hand on the doorknob and her right hand closed against the dried yellow petals of agrimony. Only when she was certain that her cousin was sleeping soundly, did she move to the bed and place the flowers beneath Imara's pillow. Her lips moved silently and Nilah reached out to touch her cousin's curls, a slight smile playing across her lips. Nilah left the room, certain that her cousin would remain asleep until well after sunrise.

Singly, or in groups of two or three, people left the house, until just two women sleeping deeply remained. One was disturbed by dreams of longing and approaching loneliness The hallway remained empty except for the slight breeze that played along the length of the space, yet, soft footfalls could be heard on the stairs. The breeze carried scents of pipe smoke and a hint of mint. The scent traveled on the breeze and gently pushed through the door of the front bedroom. There it once again mingled with the scent of the old woman. The woman, with a deep inhale, dreamed her husband with her again. A small wheeze in slumber and she moved beneath the thin bed sheet to accommodate her partner. Her forehead furrowed in disagreement and a moment later smoothed. Another deep inhalation and exhalation and she was at rest.

Rather than sleeping soundly as she was supposed to, Imara's slumber was upset by a stomach that was too full. She rolled onto her stomach, and awoke. Still more asleep than awake, Imara opened her eyes slightly and tried to place where she was. She thought she had been awakened by the sound of drumming or laughter or both. She tried to make out sounds, but all she could hear were crickets. The sound was so loud she thought crickets were in the room with her. Her limbs felt leaden. She struggled to move off of her stomach and turn to her side. The air was oppressive, weighing her down and kept her pinned to the bed. The sheet beneath her head and neck was damp with sweat. She thought maybe she was still asleep, the dark so complete she couldn't tell whether her eyes were open or closed. Imara had had dreams like this before. She would try to manipulate the dream and move in ways she couldn't when awake. Sometimes she flew and felt so free. Sometimes she flew.

She lay there asleep-awake, awake and dreaming. She felt a pop and pull. Looking back at her body on the bed. The bed with its soft white sheets. The bed with the body lying there, the eyes half closed, half opened, her eyes, her dream-eyes. With those dream-eyes she peered out the window. Now she was at the window. No need to move the curtain with her dream-hands. She saw a little further with her dream-eyes. She saw the figures beyond the lake, beyond and through the trees. Trees festooned with Spanish moss. A group in a shape. A group, a circle.

The figures dancing, moving in slow motion dream-Imara saw. With hearing that wasn't hearing she made out the beat of drums that she dream-thought she'd heard. Low, slow and throbbing, drums. Bodies came together and parted, an ancient precursor to dance. Elemental dance, the bodies slow, now fast, moving together, in pairs. The air laden with moisture and more, on the air a scent of burning, smoldering, a fire, drums, bodies, scent of herbs, burning, flames, licking the moist wood, the flames, joining and parting, reaching higher, dying down, low, the bodies, together, and higher, arms skyward and moving, low, sweeping low, moving the fire, around the fire. And the beat. The beat moving the bodies, bodies with the beat and the heat and the drums , the fire, moving the bodies, and the heat and the beat.

Dream-Imara watched without eyes. Dream-Imara watched with understanding. She reached outward, toward the half-glimpsed gathering. Dream-Imara must have called out, made a sound, without lips to move, made a sound without lungs to breathe. Some turned toward the sound, toward the house. Dream-Imara retreated. Reaching toward the ceiling with her mind that was awake and not asleep, floating over the bed. A pull and a tug from that body on the bed. The two became one and Imara shifted in sleep.

At a time close to dawn, a too full bladder awakened Imara. She felt groggy, and wondered for a moment where she was. She recalled she was in North Carolina. In a room that felt stifling. She felt hot and sticky from the perspiration drying on her neck. They were here for the funeral of her great-uncle Brownlee. She rose slowly and sat on the side of the bed. She reached out with her toes to find the slippers she thought she'd left by the bed. She found one slipper and when her toes couldn't locate the other one, decided to forego it and shuffled toward the door. Her head felt hot and sticky and full, the fullness pulling down on her eyes, making her neck felt stiff, much worse than the two glasses of wine she had should warrant. Assisted by the moonlight streaming through the window, she opened the door and walked into the hallway, and turned to the right. Something unseen moved through and past her, the air chilled her sweaty body. Unbidden, the word "Brownlee," passed her lips. Staring towards the gems of light falling on the floor of the hallway, Imara looked left and squinted at the shape she saw by the stairs. Imara, felt drunk and woozy and tried to stand still. She didn't understand or believe what she was witnessing. She looked toward the stained glass window and then looked to the left again and she saw that she was alone in the hallway. Nothing and no one in the house moved, all its occupants were quiet.

Imara felt shaken and slightly confused. She made her way to the bathroom. The glare from the light sent a shard of pain through her head and she peed and washed her hands with one eye closed. She avoided looking in the mirror above the sink.She didn't want to half-see anything that might be reflected in the mirror.

Imara left the bathroom and made it back to her room without further sightings. She climbed back into the bed, and pulled the covers over her shoulder and succumbed to sleep almost immediately.

Morning arrived and Imara was awakened by the sound of dozens of birds calling, cawing and announcing a new day. Imara took a moment to orient herself, again remembering that she was in North Carolina for her great-uncle's funeral. She guessed the reason for her slight headache was one glass too many from the night before coupled with the torturously long train ride. Despite the headache that was situated right over her left eye, Imara felt strangely rested. The air felt both heavy and fresh this morning, and Imara breathed in deeply. She stretched fully, enjoying the feel of the sheets against her skin. They had the soft feel that only comes with age and quality and Imara decided the day could wait a little longer and turned to her side to listen to the birdsong. Despite the headache, Imara realized she felt good, she felt relaxed.

She must have fallen back to sleep because Imara was awakened by a light knocking on the door. Waking reluctantly, she said, "Come in," pulling the sheet up to her neck. She was greeted by Nilah's smiling face peeking in the door, "Good mornin', ohh, I'm sorry, I woke you, I don't know why, I thought you were awake. That must have been a tiring train ride."

"What time is it? Did I oversleep?"

"It's nine in the mornin', and for us, it might as well be three o'clock," Nilah said, one hand on her hip the other on the doorknob. This morning Nilah was dressed in a long loose skirt, in pale grey and a simple white t-shirt that showed off her toned upper arms. Her silver bracelets covered the first three inches of her lower arm from her wrist and long oval silver earrings decorated her ears. Nilah was tall and imposing looking. Her medium brown face was crowned by long dreadlocks that reached mid-back. She had the ageless look so common to the women in the family. Good genes were how it was always explained, when someone commented on the fact that the women didn't begin to show their ages until they were very old, like Aunt Ora, or Nawnie. But even then, they could be anywhere from eighty years old or one hundred, their faces never told the truth of their ages.

Now that Imara had a moment to look at her Southern cousin, she came to a realization.

"Oh wow, you remind me of Nawnie! I was wondering who it was, and it just came to me," Imara said, sitting up in bed.

"That's funny, you remind me of Nawnie too, but, it's not the way you look, it's something else. Oh, well, just proves were fam'ly." With that both women let out a loud laugh.

"I better get out of this bed, or y'all will think I'm a lazy bum." Imara got out of the bed, and started to straighten the covers. "Oh, leave that, we have a woman who comes in. If you make your bed, she'll get all upset. Come on downstairs."

Imara left the room and the herbs that Nilah had left under her pillow the night before to insure her deep sleep.

Breakfast was no less confusing than the introductions the night before. There were still too many people to keep track of and Chike and Cat were deep in conversation with others. They were unavailable to help Imara through the maze of names and smiling faces. She looked for Aunt Ora at the table but didn't see her. *She's probably been up and puttering around for hours, old people can never sleep in,* Imara thought as she picked at what had to be a homemade biscuit. The biscuit had density and weight to it; no flaky quasi-croissant, this biscuit had heft. "Oh my goodness these biscuits are good. Who made them?"

A woman who Imara knew she had been introduced to at least twice, (*was her name Jovan, Kada?*) answered, "Oh, that's Baby's recipe, she makes the best biscuits, don't she?"

"Mmm hmm," Imara looked around the room for Baby. "Is she here?" "Yeah, she's in the kitchen, probably startin' lunch."

Imara got up and walked toward the kitchen. As she was pushing through the swinging half doors, a woman burst into the dining room. "Mama's dead." Her face was a rictus of grief. Imara looked over at Chike and then Cat, with a look that said, *Is this for real?*

Imara got out of the way as the closer relatives of Aunt Ora set the death machine in motion. Calls were made, an ambulance came and Aunt Ora's remains were retired to the funeral home. The gathered relatives then were able to pick up the litany of "Well, at least she died at home," and "She jus' didn't want to go on without Uncle Brownlee", "That's how it is with the old ones, they been together so long, they jus' can't live without each other", "Ain't that something? How they both died, and now everybody is already here?"

Chike and Cat took care to call home and let the rest of the family know about the latest death. Imara didn't know Ora, she'd seemed like a nice lady, but she didn't know if she would call it a tragedy, the woman was *old.* Imara decided to take the time while everyone else was distracted to explore the grounds. She walked into the hallway heading back to her room to dress and passed two women sitting on the stairs, with their arms around each other consoling one another. "I'm sorry sorry for your loss," Imara said, feeling awkward as she passed them to continue on her way to her room. As she got to the second floor landing, she saw a woman carrying bedsheets coming out of her bedroom. *They change the sheets everyday? Like in a hotel? Huh,*

Imara thought to herself. She didn't want to disturb the woman cleaning her room, so she stood awkwardly in the hall, waiting for her to finish. She didn't even have her phone in her robe pocket so she couldn't distract herself with work or play while waiting so she took the time to take a look at the third floor.

Imara took the stairs to the third floor landing and was surprised that the third floor appeared as large and wide as the second floor. There was a stained glass window on this level also, only set toward the front of the house. Most of the doors were open, and she could tell they were being occupied by out of town guests, by the suitcases in the rooms set on beds or chairs. She was struck by how filled with light the third floor was, no gloomy close attic here. At the end of the hallway there were two doors that were closed. Imara found herself reaching toward the doorknob until her better manners took hold. *You'd hate it if someone visiting you decided to snoop around and open doors.* After chastising herself thoroughly, Imara walked to the end of the hallway and made her way back to the second floor and to her room. She imagined the cleaning lady was finished in there by now.

She spied the small woman in Aunt Ora's room as she passed. She was stripping the sheets from that bed too. The woman, who looked to be in her mid-forties, looked up from her work as Imara passed.

"Good mornin'. I changed your sheets. If you need anything, just let me know, I'm Baby." "Oh, thank you. Oh, you're Baby, I wanted to tell you this morning, you know, before…that your biscuits were delicious. I'd love the recipe," Imara said. The woman, beamed over her sheet filled arms. "Oh, I'm glad you liked them. It's not going to be the same 'round here without Miss Ora and Mister Brownlee." "Had you worked for them long?" Imara asked, leaning in the doorway. "I worked for them for 'bout twenty years, my Momma worked for them all her life. Ain't too many black folks around here that had help, 'specially in those days. But, you know, your family, they special, always have been. It's nice, working for them, they treat you like fam'ly."

Imara smiled and told Baby *(Miss Baby?)* she'd see her later. There were a few well-to-do black families that she had encountered in college, but their wealth was newer than her family's. She had never really questioned the fact that the entire family was well off. It was just a fact, like the fact that they aged well or usually employed only family members. It was simply how things were done. When the time came to decide what you wanted to do with your life, the family was there to help you get your idea off the ground. Imara just thought it was wise to keep the money in the family and hadn't thought about it much beyond that.

Imara was pleased to find that the bathroom was free, so she quickly showered and dressed for the day. She wanted to get outside and take a look at the grounds. She was intrigued by the idea that the house was basically a peninsula, with the waterfront to the front and that lake in the back. Dressing in a lightweight cotton skirt in lavender and a purple t-shirt, with black sandals and pushing her hands through her curly 'fro to reposition it into a less wild style, Imara was ready. She quickly checked her phone to see if she had any messages or frantic emails from Marla and was struck by the fact that it had been hours since she'd even thought about *Imara's Kitchen*. She also noticed that her shoulders weren't hunched up around her ears. Edenton was having a positive effect on her stress levels, even if people were dropping like flies. Seeing nothing urgent on her phone, she left the phone on the dresser and walked downstairs.

When she came upon Deon and Nilah in the living room, and because she felt she knew them better than the others, Imara stopped in the room and asked if there was anything she could do to help with the funeral arrangements. They answered in the negative, which meant Imara was free to get outside. She didn't see Chike or Cat anywhere, and thought that since they were more familiar with the town, that maybe they were actually being useful to the family by running errands.

Imara walked into the kitchen and out the back door. There was a back porch that ran the length of the house and there were wicker chairs, lounges and tables at each end. A wide set of stairs led to the lawn and beyond that the lake. The lake was overhung with cypress trees which were draped with Spanish moss, in all its silvery green glory. Imara was struck by the quiet beauty of the scene. She stood at the top of the steps and just looked around and breathed deeply. As she looked across to the other side of the water, she half-remembered a snippet of a dream from the night before. The dream had music and dancing, like a party, and then the snippet was gone. Looking around Imara noticed what she hadn't the night before. There were no other houses around that she could see. The house sat alone on this tract of land and there was nothing across the water either. Imara walked down the steps and walked to the right. She got a better look at the lake and saw that she'd been wrong. There was something across the water. It looked like a small cemetery. She wondered if it was a family cemetery, she couldn't see if there was a church attached to it, but she wouldn't have been surprised if there was, a family church of course.

Enjoying the warm sunlight and how it reflected on the water, Imara felt at peace. She sat on the bottom step so that she could feel the heat that was soaking into the earth through the soles of her sandals. There was a fresh smell to the air but also a heaviness to it that wasn't fresh, necessarily, but had substance. There was no chance of anyone moving quickly in Edenton. The air had substance and weight and was a factor in every decision you made in where you were going and how you got there. The water made slight sounds as it lapped against the shore. When Imara looked to the left she noticed the pier and the boats that were tied up to it. That solved the mystery of how people got to the other shore. Even having a boat as a mode of transportation was a world away from how fast things moved in Philly. The idea that she might want a summer home in a place like Edenton, if not in Edenton itself began to nibble at her brain. What she had seen of the town when they'd driven through last night was like something out of another century. *It might be nice to* *have a small place that had a view of the water,*Imara thought. Then she remembered that she didn't take vacations and that having it as a summer home in a swamp wasn't necessarily the smartest idea in the world. It would make more sense to migrate south in the winter. As much as she loved Philly, traveling through the city in the winter was an exercise in patience. She often found herself screaming at the other drivers (to herself. If she actually screamed out loud at the other drivers, that would be like asking to be shot. In the face. *Ah, Philly, gotta love it.*

For now, the idea was an idle one, thinking *how nice it would be to step outside and see the water, having a cup of coffee on a balcony, letting the warm, heavy air push against her brow, feeling the sun beating down on her shoulders,*feeling the heat in this quiet, pretty, wild place. These were the daydreams she was entertaining when her cousin Cat came around the side of the house and found her.

"There you are. We were looking for you. Chike and I have to drop the obituary off at the newspaper, want to come see this one-horse town?"

"Yes," Imara said, standing and stretching lazily. "Let me go get my bag."

Imara went back into the house through the kitchen and was greeted by Miss Baby's smiling face. You could tell that Baby ran a tight ship in the kitchen, she had prep bowls at the ready and the counters were filled with various components of many dishes, but the area was spotless.

"I'm sorry to walk through, I need to go up and get my bag," Imara said as she made her way towards the swinging doors. "Oh, that's alright. You can take the back stairs too," Baby said inclining her head towards the staircase that Imara had completely bypassed. "Thanks, lunch smells delicious." Imara loved nothing better than the aroma of sauteeing garlic and onions and the kitchen was perfumed by the scents.

The acrid scent of white sage struck her when she reached the second floor. Imara figured that someone, most likely Baby, had been smudging incense after Aunt Ora's body had been removed. She was very familiar with the practice, her Aunt Sweetie was known to smudge whenever anyone she didn't like had set foot in Covington House back at home. She said it the practice of smudging removed the negative energy from a space. She also claimed it had origins in Native American tribes, which she also claimed Nawnie was a member of the Algonquin tribe. Imara didn't know how much to believe, but she was familiar with the scent of sage its sharp scent.

Imara made sure to actually pick up her phone and drop it in her bag and checked in the mirror to make sure her hair, which could manage to be unruly on the best of days, was still reasonably presentable. Pressing down one side and fluffing up the other, she and her 'fro were ready to see the sights of Edenton.

CHAPTER THREE

Homegoing

With Chike at the wheel, Cat in the back seat and Imara in the front passenger seat, they set off for what ended up being the center of town. Imara was again struck by how pretty the town was. Highlighted by homes painted white and light colored brickwork, there were even white picket fences fronting some of the homes. She saw people walking their dogs, and stopping to chat on the corners. The residential area, which was small, had copious gardens lush and overflowing with shrubs and flowering plants. Blooms of every color, a riotous blend of white, yellow and pink blossoms bordered every home.

Within minutes they came to the main street, Broad Street and Imara had to laugh. "Nothing like Broad Street at home is it?" Back in Philly, Broad Street was a wide thoroughfare with four lanes of traffic that ran north and south through most of the large city. In contrast, here in Edenton, Broad Street was two blocks long and a two lane street. It was *broader* than the surrounding streets, but, that was the only resemblance to the Broad Street Imara was familiar with from Philly.

"No, you have to take the name with a grain of salt." Chike said. "But, isn't it pretty here, I love coming back, it's like another world" Cat said, looking left and right as they slowed in front of a storefront. "Yes, it's beautiful. I was just thinking how nice it would be to have a small place down here to come in the winter."

"Oh! We should totally do that, get a place and share it, that way we can rotate weekends or whatever and just have a hideaway," Cat said, immediately warming to the idea.

Chike said as they got out of the car, "Cat, check the listings while we're here, the property should be dirt cheap." Imara was starting to get excited by the prospect of owning a little waterfront property down south. "Are y'all serious? You really want to do this?" Imara grinned. *This is going to happen, I can feel it.* Even thought she'd only been in Edenton less than 24 hours, she loved what she had seen and experienced in the town so far.

Chike held the door open for his cousins and they walked into the dark newspaper office. Inside two people were sitting behind desks, one on each side of the partition that ran along both sides of the room. The other two desks were empty. There was a frosted glass door at the far end of the room that announced **Editor** in big, black bold letters. Chike, with his normal impatience, cleared his throat after not being acknowledged immediately. The woman sitting to the right of the door looked up with a slight smile, which disappeared when she saw the three people standing at the partition. "Can I help you?" she asked, clearly not wanting to help at all.

Chike raised an eyebrow at the chilly reception and said, "Yes, yes you can. We have an obituary notice for tomorrow's paper and my cousin would like to see your real estate listings. Current ones."

Imara was momentarily confused by the reception and then chalked it up to silly, racist, white people. Coming from the north and Philadelphia in particular, it was easy to forget that there were white people who hated blacks on principle. That was not enough to change her mind or dampen her excitement over the idea of buying a house in Edenton.

The woman was old, thankfully, her generation was dying out and would be replaced by a generation of white people who lived in a world that was increasingly more brown than pink.

The man who shared the space with "Racist Sally", as Imara had dubbed her spoke up. "I can show you the real estate listings." Cat and Imara turned in his direction and Imara noticed that admiring glance that he gave to her voluptuous cousin. It was a look that Imara was used to Cat receiving from members of the opposite sex, and sometimes from the same sex. Cat was sexy. Dressed in her "bummy clothes" of cutoff shorts and a shirt tied at her waist, with no makeup except lip gloss on her full lips she was still sexy. Cat looked like a real life brown Barbie doll, with an impossible figure and a huge head of hair. Also, Cat had a way of looking that made people, men in particular, putty in her hands.

"Great. Let's see those listings." That was the other thing about Cat, when she decided to turn it on, everything she said was a double entendre. The man showing them the listings was not immune to her charms, Imara noticed that his neck was turning decidedly pink above his shirt collar. He pulled out a binder and placed it on the counter in front of them.

"Are you ladies in the market for a big or a small house in town?" he asked making conversation and directing his question at Imara, who he obviously felt safer talking to.

"Oh, we don't know yet, we were thinking about something on the water." "Ah, well, I'll direct you to Ruth Simmons, she handles most of the waterfront properties in town. Her office is right down the street. But you're welcome to look in the paper while you wait for your...?" he asked, looking over toward Chike. "Cousin," Imara answered. With that, the man, who was balding with a larger than small paunch, and didn't stand a chance on a good day, stood a little straighter. He pulled out another binder with the last month's real estate listings and Imara was once again reminded that she wasn't in Philly anymore. She and Cat bent over the ads, when the man behind the counter got up the nerve to ask a question, "So, are you all just movin' to town? Where you from?" "No, we're looking for a vacation place, mainly. We all live in Philadelphia," Cat answered.

"Oh, well now, how'd you hear about Edenton? It's not exactly a big tourist spot. Although it sure should be. Do ya know people here?" he asked.

"Yes, we have family here, the Wards. Our great uncle and aunt just died. Our Aunt Ora Ward actually just died today." Imara answered. She was looking at the binder at a house that had promise, so she missed the look of fear that passed over the man's face. Some of the color that had risen suddenly drained from his face and fleshy jowls. But, Cat didn't, and she made a point to smile at the man, which only made him blanch more, if that was possible. Now his visage had a grayish tinge. "Let me know if ya need any help," he said, going back to his desk and pretending to look at his computer monitor.

By this time Chike was finished with the obituary and they left the newspaper office. Imara wanted to walk down Broad Street to get a feel for the very small town, so that's what they did. Imara didn't know if it was the August heat or because it was the middle of the afternoon, but the street was practically empty. They passed one or two people out running errands. The quiet of the town was unnerving, there weren't even ambient sounds really. If she strained her ears, Imara was certain she could hear the water from the river, which was five minutes away from where they were walking. After stopping in the little grocery store, to get ice cream, they walked back to the rental car. What they didn't notice was the number of people in the shops who were watching their progress back to their car and the collective sigh of relief when they drove off.

When they got back to the house, which Chike shared with Imara was called Maisie House, they were given some surprising news. There would be a double funeral, somehow the funeral home would be able to get Aunt Ora ready in time so that the family could have her funeral on the same day as Uncle Brownlee. They had missed lunch, but Baby was in the kitchen preparing dinner when they returned. Feeling most at home in the kitchen, Imara made herself comfortable on a stool. And Baby fixed her a plate from the cold roast chicken and arugula salad from lunch. Imara sat picking at the food, watching Baby move expertly around the kitchen. There would be a cobbler for dessert. Baby was busy peeling nectarines and peaches. Imara asked her if she had any family and what the town was like. Baby said she came from a small family, consisting of just her mother, father and an older sister who lived in Atlanta. Baby had never married and didn't have children, but unlike some women in her situation, she didn't sound apologetic, it was all said in a very matter of fact way. She didn't have anything to compare the town to, never having lived anywhere else besides Edenton. Imara felt close to Baby, somehow, they had more in common than she felt with her cousins, who were all very gregarious and fun loving. It seemed to be a family trait, a trait that seemed to have skipped over Imara altogether. Somehow in the course of conversation she said something along those lines to Baby and Baby said,

"Oh, you're like your mother like that, she was quiet too." Imara's ears immediately perked up at mention of her mother. Without realizing it, Imara held her breath for a moment. It was seldom that anyone mentioned either of her parents.To hear this woman in Edenton, North Carolina, of all places, so far from home mention Essie, was startling.

"You knew my mother?" Imara asked when she had collected herself. "Oh yes, she was a nice lady, very nice, I knew her, she was from here, so yes, uh huh I knew her,"Baby said as she mixed the wet ingredients in with the dry for her cobbler dough.

Nilah came into the kitchen, saying, "Come on outside with us, we're gonna to cool off from this heat." And that was how the next few days were spent while waiting for the double funeral. Lazy days spent swimming in the lake during the day or taking the boat out in the evening, making lazy circuits around the property. Rather than a somber time, she was having a great time, it was just the respite that Imara needed from work. It was so relaxing that she needed to remind herself to check in daily with Marla and Charlotte about how things were going with her business.

Before she knew it the day of the funeral had arrived. The house was more crowded than normal, even before they took the short drive to the church.

Imara's suspicions were right, the church attached to the small cemetery was a family church. The pastor was another relative as were most of the members of the congregation. There was a way to get to the church without going by boat and the procession to the church took the long way around.

The church was a small red brick affair with a modest interior. So small, that the pews were packed with people paying their respects in sardine-like seatings. Imara was glad that the first two pews were reserved for family otherwise they may not have had a seat. At one point during the eulogy for Uncle Brownlee, Imara turned around and was surprised to see that it really was standing room only in the church. From the look of things, the Ward double funeral was a big deal in Edenton. Those paying their respects seemed to include the entire town, among the black as well as the white residents. One obvious non-family member caught her eye as she was scanning the church in her boredom. He was tall, with dark hair, and a wide jaw. He seemed to be staring right at her when she happened to look toward the back of the church. When she held his gaze for a moment he had the decency to at least look down. Imara turned her attention back to the funeral and the service.

After the church service they took the short walk around the church to the cemetery where there was an even shorter service. The air was still. There was a strong threat of storms later in the day.Imara was distracted by the fact that she could see Maisie House across the water. She was not looking forward to the procession coming back to the house for what she always called the funeral after-party. These things typically lasted for hours and ended with people drunk-crying and telling stories about the dead that painted them as saints or sinners, usually saints. Since the deceased were so old, the stories were likely to veer in the saintly vein, because no one was still around that knew them when they were young enough to be sinners.

Imara wanted nothing more than to sneak away and maybe lie out beside the water and take a nap. The past two days, she, Chike and Cat had looked at three waterfront properties, but nothing had been exactly what they were looking for. The properties either needed too much work, or were those horrible McMansions with no character and vaulted ceilings or were two small should the three of them ever decide to come down all at once.

Imara looked at Maisie house and realized it was perfect, if just slightly too big for the three of them, for a vacation home. That and the fact that it wasn't for sale. She didn't know which of her relatives would get the house after the estate was settled, but maybe they could ask to stay there on occasion. Everyone had been so friendly, she had a feeling she might get a yes in response to her question.

The funeral after party was a surprisingly festive affair. There was more food than Imara had seen in a long time, which was an impressive feat, since she was a caterer. She had no idea when Baby could have prepared half of the food let alone most of it. Obviously, she'd had help, a lot of it.

Also, even though it was early afternoon, the booze was flowing. The people in attendance weren't shy and were imbibing like there was no tomorrow. Now Imara realized why there weren't very many cars blocking the driveway. These people had come prepared to drink, so they had walked to the church from their homes and taken the long walk around the lake to the house after the burial.

As the booze flowed, the tongues loosened as was normally the case, at one of these affairs. Imara, knowing only a handful of people kept to the corners and watched the action, putting that half-smile on her face that's supposed to convey "Hi, I'm pleasant, but don't know you, let's not talk, okay?" For the most part the look worked, but then she was cornered by an old woman who wanted to engage in conversation. The old woman was sharp-witted at least,and had made Imara chuckle a few times. She was staring up at Imara now with her watery brown eyes.

"So, whose daughter are you? I know most of the Wards, I don't think I've seen you before. Where you live, baby?"

Imara was in the process of changing her mind about the sharp wit of the old lady. She'd answered this question of parentage a couple of times already and as the day dragged on, her patience dissipated. As she looked around to see what she could do to make an escape, she was rescued by one of her male Ward cousins, who came by to ask Imara for help in the kitchen.

Imara excused herself and whispered up to Jovan, "Thank you," holding on to his arm as they made their way to the kitchen.

"No problem, cuz, I can never remember her name, but she is annoying."

They chuckled as they walked into the kitchen which surprisingly, was an oasis of calm. Rather than the hordes of helpers that Imara expected to see, it was just Baby and another woman who where talking quietly by the counter at the back of the large kitchen. Every available space on the counter was covered with a dish. There were meatballs, chicken kabobs, mini quiches, sushi, slices of at least four different cakes, platters of shrimp, mushrooms stuffed with crab, catfish poppers, little spoonfuls of baked macaroni and cheese, a smorgasbord of flavors and tastes.

Baby, looking over at them, asked "Do y'all need somethin', our we out of somethin', what do I need to brang out?" Jovan answered, "No, I was jus' rescuin' Imara from that lady, what's her name, she always wears them big purple hats to church?"

Smiling, Baby said "Miss Brown. I always call her Miss. Purple that woman sure loves purple, not just hats either, but her name Miss Brown. I bet she got a purple scarf or bag or belt on right now."

Unable to resist, Imara and Jovan went to the swinging doors and looked through the crack trying to locate Mrs. Brown in the crowd. They were rewarded by a sighting of purple, off to the left. "Oh, wow, that is too funny." Imara and Jovan turned and laughed at the sight of Mrs. Brown and her purple sash that was wrapped around where her waist would have been.

"Okay, I can't hide in here all day, can I take one of these trays out, Miss Baby?" Imara looked over at the woman leaning against the counter. *She must be exhausted, she's probably been on her feet all day and half the night putting this together,* Imara thought. Baby looked over and smiled a tired smile, "Thank you."

Imara and Jovan went back into the formal dining room, removed several empty trays and made the trip back to the kitchen. After several more trips back and forth the buffet was replenished and Imara was snacking from her plate of mushroom

111

caps when she realized she had been listening in on a whispered conversation happening behind her.

"Ah course the money and the house is goin' to Tanessa and Jovan, all they kids is dead, it's jus' the grandkids now."

"That was strange, both they kids died like that."

"Ain't nothing strange 'bout it, if you know like I do. You know the story right? How both they kids drown? They always was somethin' 'bout the Ward kids anyway, if you know what I mean. They was real close."

"You better not let them hear you, somethin' happen to you next. I'm going to get me some more baked macaroni and cheese. God bless her, Baby sure put her foot in it for Miss Ora and Mister Brownlee, din't she?"

With that the two women walked toward the buffet to fill their plates again and Imara got a good look at them. She must have been staring because one of the women, the older of the two, looked back and caught Imara's eye. Something spooked her because her face dropped as her eyes widened and she brought her hand to her neck in a protective gesture.

In the next room, the crying had begun which meant that the drinking had moved into the serious territory and people were getting drunk. As a result, the gathering was getting louder and Imara wanted desperately to get away. When she made her next circuit around the room she slipped through the French doors leading to the deck. Imara was moving quickly and looking behind her instead of in front so when she walked into the wall of flesh she shouldn't have been surprised but was.

"Oh god, I'm so sorry," she said as she bent to pick up mushroom caps that had spilled off her plate and on to the decking. The man she had bumped into was the same one she'd felt staring at her during the church service. Now his face was inches from hers and she had a chance to look at him more closely. His face was broad, with wrinkles lining his forehead and crow's feet surrounding his pale hazel eyes. When she had first noticed him in the church, she had immediately placed him as a random white guy because his very pale coloring and sandy brown curly hair had made him stand apart from the sea of brown hued mourners. Now that they were sharing the same airspace, she saw that he was obviously mixed. His features, the larger, wider, nose and full lips placing him on the blacker side of the racial scale. She thought his face not unattractive but not her usual taste, which tended toward the darker skinned men. But the way he held her gaze and seemed to look at and through her was enough to make her uncomfortable in a pleasant way. There was a tug that felt a little like a heart thud and Imara realized she was holding her breath. She broke the stare by looking down, searching for more runaway mushroom caps.

"I think we got them all," Tall, Not so Dark and Handsome said, placing mushrooms on her plate and wiping his hands together.

"Yep," was all Imara could think to say, looking anywhere but at him. "Oh, here's a napkin."

"Thanks," he said, wiping his hands on the napkin and then placing it on the plate Imara was holding.

"How do you.." Before he could finish the sentence Imara had turned on her heel and walked toward the kitchen. Guy shook his head and walked back toward the deck railing.

Imara placed the plate on the counter and without even clearing it, walked up the back stairs to the second floor. She told herself she needed to use the bathroom, but really just needed some time to collect herself. In the bathroom she looked at her face in the mirror. *What was that?* She asked herself and got no answer from the reflection in the mirror. She stared into her own eyes to gain her composure and felt her breathing slow. Falling into a meditative state as she gazed into the mirror, her eyes unfocused now, she was brought back to the present when she thought she saw something standing behind her in the mirror. She gave a startled "What the," and turned quickly, thinking maybe someone had come into the room while she was zoned out looking at herself in the mirror. Nothing and no one stood behind her. Turning on the cold water, Imara splashed some on her face and tried to slow her breathing again. Thinking that she was just tired, that maybe the humidity was starting to get to her or that she'd had too much to drink and not enough to eat *and thanks to the Wall of Man she'd walked into, she'd lost her mushroom caps,* Imara decided to brave the first floor again to get some real food.

Stopping in her room to check her phone for any messages from home, from Marla or Charlotte about the business, she saw a message from Marla.

Everything is fine here no need to worry

Imara chuckled to herself and put the phone back on the dresser. Marla had a way of answering questions before she was asked, it was a knack she had. Imara was glad they were so close that Marla could read her mind even from this distance. Thinking that enough time had passed since she'd embarrassed herself with the strange guy, Imara made her way back downstairs by way of the back stairs so she could get food and maybe eat without being disturbed.

Most of the older people had left; the town mourners, the people that had known Brownlee and Ora through church and from being lifelong residents of Edenton. What was left was mainly family and it had really turned into a party by this time. The living room looked like a hurricane had struck it - there were glasses and plates strewn everywhere and people were starting to drape and fold themselves over the furniture after a full afternoon of drinking and eating hor dourves.

After stopping in the kitchen to fill her plate, Imara walked into the living room and noticed a woman sitting in the corner in a wingback chair, drunk-sobbing, bent over in the chair, while the man standing to her side consoled her, patting her on the back, saying over and over again "I know, I know". Walking through the dining room heading toward the deck again, *No, she was not looking for that guy again, he was long gone, she was looking for Cat or Chike,* she told herself, she saw Chike sitting at the dining room table talking to Deon and Jovan. Imara half-remembered snippets from the half-overheard conversation from earlier, something about Jovan and his cousin being left everything and how their parents had died...It was hazy in her mind, but she wanted to remember to ask Chike or Cat later on when they were alone.

As was the habit of her family when more than two or more were gathered the laughter was not far behind. The group from the dining room made their way to the deck and then spilled down to the bank of the lake. Someone got the idea to take the boat out onto the water and Imara hopped in. She was struck by how beautiful the swamp looked in the moonlight, with the moss hanging down moving slowly in the heavy breeze that would stir once in a while. The trees reflected their shape on the water, their silhouettes broken by the paddling of the oars. Jovan was working the oars, and Imara was leaning back on her elbows, completely relaxed.

"Oh, god, it's so beautiful here, I see why people never leave," Imara said to no one in particular. Jovan smiled in the dark, making a lazy circuit of the lake. Looking toward the other shore, Imara saw a couple walking in the cemetery, but couldn't tell from this distance if it was part of their party. She didn't see a boat on the other shore, but it could have been pulled up beyond where she could see.

"It's probably Granpop and Granma," Jovan said matter-of-factly to Imara's unasked question.

"Ha, yeah, probably," Imara laughed until she looked over at Jovan and saw he was serious. Somehow the idea that they were talking about the recently deceased while canoeing on a swamp across from a graveyard in the moonlight, seemed perfectly normal here in Edenton and Imara relaxed back in the boat, allowing the warm air to brush over her skin.

After a time, Jovan pulled up to the opposite shore and pulled the canoe up onto the sand. Imara, feeling lazy in the humidity, didn't want to move. She continued to lay back in the canoe, listening to the night sounds as she watched Jovan walk toward the graveyard. She could see that several people, not just the shadow couple she'd spied earlier were walking through the small graveyard, talking softly, walking in groups of two or three. Imara stayed outside of the scene, keeping as an observer. Her senses heightened and contracted at the same time. The warm, thick air muffled conversations, so she only heard the murmurs of conversations, but she picked up a rhythm all the same.

Her eyes closed, she took in what her other senses were picking up. She could hear the water lapping against the canoe, she thought she could even hear footfalls as they made their way over the damp earth in the graveyard. There were the sounds of mosquitoes and other humming insects and the air was filled with cricket song. The smell of the swamp was green and sweet with the stench of rot below the surface, telling the story of life and death and beyond.

Imara must have dozed off because the sound of a drum being beat with one hand sliding over the skin woke her. The waking was slow and soft, her head feeling dense with drink and heat. She was sticky and creaky and realized she didn't want to awaken fully, instead preferring to stay in limbo, between wake and sleep, committing to neither, one foot in both worlds. When she opened her eyes she immediately wanted to close them again. The scene in the cemetery was too foreign, too familiar, too much to take in all at once.

The family had formed a loose circle around what had to be the fresh graves of Aunt Ora and Uncle Brownlee. Imara, feeling a weight on her shoulders, got out of the canoe to get a closer look at the gathering. She had a feeling of dread about what she was witnessing and the dread had more to do with missing out than participating, she realized.

Walking toward the group, she saw there was a small fire near the where the gravestones for her aunt and uncle would be, off to the side her cousin, Dravin, was beating a drum slowly.

All at once Imara realized that everything that had transpired earlier today had been a farce, a play, a show for the town. This, right here, in this swamp, this was the actual home-going ceremony. Family, gathered, swaying together, susurrus of a song she couldn't make out or maybe it was just individual prayers to the dead for the dead, Imara didn't know. She joined the swaying, feeling the energy of those gathered to send Ora and

Brownlee, who they had been, who they were, their true faces to the shadow lands. This felt right, this felt natural to her. When the drum beat a little faster she, like the others, responded, moving faster in time to the drumbeat. Moving in time to the sound of the drum, which followed a throbbing in her bones, in her blood, she moved. It was more than dance, it was less than dance, it was committing these bodies to the earth, committing their souls to what was next, what was always waiting always present and just out of sight. They danced in the moonlight, in a circle in pairs, in groups of three, there were arms raised, bodies swung low. Imara felt alive as she honored the dead.

What felt like hours later the gathering broke up, the spell was broken, the drum was silenced and they made their way across the swamp, headed to their beds, their duty to the ancestors done.

End Part One.

www.ingramcontent.com/pod-product-compliance
Lightning Source LLC
Chambersburg PA
CBHW060440130626
46555CB00005B/2442